MIGHTY MIKE
BUILDS A Library

By Kelly Lynch   Illustrated by Casey Lynch

magic
wagon

visit us at www.abdopublishing.com

For Madalyn —KL
For Lucy —CL

Published by Magic Wagon, a division of the ABDO Group, 8000 West 78th Street, Edina, Minnesota 55439. Copyright © 2011 by Abdo Consulting Group, Inc. International copyrights reserved in all countries.

Looking Glass Library™ is a trademark and logo of Magic Wagon.

Printed in the United States of America, North Mankato, Minnesota.
092010
012011

Written by Kelly Lynch
Illustrations by Casey Lynch
Edited by Stephanie Hedlund and Rochelle Baltzer
Cover and interior layout and design by Abbey Fitzgerald

Library of Congress Cataloging-in-Publication Data

Lynch, Kelly, 1976-
  Mighty Mike builds a library / by Kelly Lynch ; illustrated by Casey Lynch.
        p. cm. -- (Mighty Mike)
  ISBN 978-1-61641-129-9
  [1. Building--Fiction. 2. Helpfulness--Fiction. 3. Community life--Fiction.] I. Lynch, Casey, ill. II. Title.
  PZ7.L9848Mbl 2011
  [E]--dc22
                                         2010016267

It was a fabulous fall morning and Mighty Mike was sitting in his office.
Mike smiled as he read about all the interesting things happening in his town.

"What?!" he suddenly yelled, jumping to his feet. "This can't be right!" But there it was, clearly written in the newspaper. The town was canceling its plans to build a new library.

Town bounces new library proposal due to insufficient funds

"Money and car keys are hard to come by these days," says Mayor.

•East Big Town- Citing budget ⁀ns, Mayor Vic Rogne has ⁀ permanent hold on the ⁀ plans to build a new ⁀rary on the corner of 3rd ⁀nd Broadway. "Has anyone seen my keys?" the Mayor is quoted as saying. Local children are very disappointed. Kenny Heidner, age 10, says, "This is going to make it hard for me to check out

E BIG TOWN GAZETTE

cal dog eats every shoe in est Big Town neighborhood

ooter especially
es basketball
es, says owner

st Big Town-
ooter, a jovial
llow labrador,
s chewed up

ery shoe in West Big Town over the last
vo weeks. "He even ate my flip flops!" said...
cont.–A8

hoe sales up in West Big own neighborhood

Im not sure why,"
ays store owner.
st Big Town–

Baseball the 'best sport', says new study

A new study,
published in The
Journal of
Baseballerino,
says baseball i
"the coolest," J.
Sinclair, the author
of the study, says.

"I just thought,
"What's the best

Mighty Mike began pacing back and forth, back and forth. *Our town needs a library,* he thought. *But what can I do? I could never build a library by myself. But, there must be a way to get it done.*

As Mighty Mike worked that morning, his mind was on the library. It was all he could think about as he cleaned and maintained his excavator.

At the end of the day, Mighty Mike realized that he couldn't build the library. Not by himself, anyway. *But,* he thought, his frown turning into a smile, *I have a lot of friends.*

Mighty Mike picked up his phone and called Carl the carpenter. "Carl, if I dig the hole, will you build the walls for the new library?" Mike asked.

"You bet," Carl quickly answered.

Next, Mighty Mike called Eric the electrician. "Eric," Mike said, "if I dig the hole and Carl the builds the walls, will you install the lights in the new library?"
"Easy," answered Eric. "You can count on me."

Finally, Mighty Mike called Pete the plumber. "Pete," Mike said, "if I dig the hole, Carl builds the walls, and Eric installs the lights, will you put the plumbing in the new library?"

"I'd be pleased to," replied Pete. Mike smiled. It looked like the town might get its library after all.

The next morning, Mighty Mike started digging the hole for the new library. As he dug, townspeople stopped to ask Mike what he was doing.

"Why, building the new library," he would answer.

When they asked how they could help, Mike scratched his head. "Well," he finally answered, "we don't have any books."

When Mighty Mike was done with the hole, Carl the carpenter built the walls. He measured each board. Then he carefully cut them and nailed them into place. As each wall went up, it looked more and more like a library.

When the walls were built and the roof was on, it was Eric the electrician's turn. He installed the outlets, switches, and lights. Soon, the library had electricity.

When Eric was done, Pete the plumber put in drinking fountains, toilets, and sinks. Now the library had water, too. All it needed were books.

While Mighty Mike and his friends were working, the townspeople had searched through their houses. They boxed up all their extra books. Now they were standing in a long line, ready to put them in their new library.

What a great day it was when the library opened! There was a big celebration with speeches and ice cream. The townspeople finally had a new library, and best of all, they'd worked together to build it. It was one of the happiest days that anyone could remember!

Glossary

cancel - to call off something without meaning to restart it.

carpenter - a worker who builds or repairs wooden structures.

electrician - a worker who sets up, maintains, and repairs electrical equipment.

excavator - a power-operated shovel.

install - to set up something for use. An installer is someone who does this.

plumber - a worker who sets up and repairs fixtures that carry water.

What Would Mighty Mike Do?

• Why does Mighty Mike decide to build the library?

• Who does Mighty Mike call to help him?

• How does Mighty Mike work together with the other people?

• How does the town feel when the library is finished?